Meet the Feeling Friends

by
Karen Cuthrell

illustrated by
Fabricio Suarez

Meet the Feeling Friends

ISBN: 1-4392-0220-6

ISBN-13: 9781439202203

Visit www.booksurge.com to order additional copies.

Meet the Feeling Friends

is dedicated to my daughter,
Lana Wesley Boone
who is my Angel
sent from Heaven,
and
Brandon Carrington Lee
who is my Angel in Heaven.

Special thanks to Geneva J. Cuthrell and John W. Cuthrell who believed in the Feeling Friends from conception!

Hugs and Kisses to The Feeling Friend Champions Who Believed!

Cheryl Avery, Lana Wesley Boone, Reginald D. Boone, Vivian Bowers, Geneva J. Cuthrell, John W. Cuthrell, Vincent Evans, Andrea Garner, Margo Hall, Angie Hersh, Pattie Hill, Thelma S. Johnson, KK's Kids, Monica Loving, Chad Marshall, Janyce Marshall, JoAnne Mussenden, S. Ann Neloms, Dr. Kathy Philyaw, Richardene Thweatt, Vincent Stovall, and Dr. Kevin Williams

I LovaRoo!
KK

Welcome to
Feeling Free Island.

My name is KK and
I want you to meet
my Feeling Friends.

My Feeling Friends
are always around you.

My Feeling Friends
are honest and true.

My Feeling Friends
are here to protect you.

My Feeling Friends
are here for YOU!

Are YOU ready to meet my Feeling Friends? Then here we GO!

My name is Lotta Love
And I'm the LovaRoo.
I LOVE expressing feelings.
I know that you will too.

Worry the Fear Worm is my name.
I WORRY and I'm nervous through and through.

If you help me to calm down,
I'll do the same for you.

I'm Angie the Angry Tiger.
I use words when I get mad.
No hitting, no pushing, no kicking, no biting.
Even when I am ANGRY,
there is never any fighting!

My name is Slumpy the Sad Elephant
And I am truly blue.
I feel like I'm SAD a lot of the time.
Do you sometimes feel that way too?

My name is Wesley the Lonely Whale.
I live in the great big blue sea.
I want to make friends with some other kids
Who are LONELY just like me.

I'm Griswald the Grumpy Grizzly
As you can plainly see.
When I am feeling GRUMPY
You better not mess with me.

My name is Flutter the Shy Butterfly.

I'm nervous about speaking out.

But in my SHY little body there is a great big voice,
And one day you will hear me shout!

Yes, I am Rant the Panic Ant.
I constantly RANT and I'm anxious as can be.
But if you will help me, I'll calm down.
Oh yes! You will see!

Hi, I'm Watcher the Caution Dog.
And I know what safety's about.
When crossing the street or playing around,
I tell everyone to watch out (WOOF, WOOF, WOOF)!

You can do it, you can do it.
I'm Ida the I-Can-Bee.
I have big dreams, and to me it seems,
Great things are waiting for me.

Happy, Lonely, Grumpy,
Caution, Panic, Worry,
Love, Shy, Sad, Angry,
Confidence, Joy,
So many feelings,
Boy, oh Boy!

You have all these feelings,
Living inside of you.
Helping you to let them out
Is what the Feeling Friends do.

Feeling Friends are always around you.
Feeling Friends are honest and true.
Feeling Friends are here to protect you.
Feeling Friends are here for you!

Did you enjoy meeting my Feeling Friends?
Remember, every feeling has its time and place.
I must respect your feelings.
You must respect my feelings!

Come back
soon to
Feeling Free
Island.

I LovaRoo!

About the Author

KK and The Feeling Friends®

Nearly fifteen years ago, KAREN D. CUTHRELL (KK) co-created the Feeling Friends as an inspired response to her young daughter's need to express inner feelings openly and honestly. Each Feeling Friend evolved as a loving guide and conduit for sharing even those sometimes hard-to-reveal emotions.

Karen's creativity and dynamic operations approach combines decades of relevant career experience in human resources for both municipal and educational organizations in the nation's capitol. She integrates her strong background in building educational and learning environments, community enrichment, and organizational viability, as the foundation for determining Feeling Friends explorations.

Karen has a true love for children. Meet the Feeling Friends is designed to help children learn to explore and express their feelings by identifying with the Feeling Friends characters. It is her hope that KK and The Feeling Friends will entertain, educate, excite and touch the child within us all. Donn B. Murphy, Ph.D, President and Executive Director of the National Theatre in Washington, DC states that KK's "performance sizzles with warmth and imagination, and brings greatly needed messages of love and hope to children." KK and her Feeling Friends are strong advocates for social emotional learning - the retrenching of fundamental character tools and skills required to thrive in today's culture.

It is Karen's purpose and dream that the Feeling Friends give children the opportunity to achieve their personal best and develop a social and emotional foundation that will help them become knowledgeable and responsible citizens in their community.

About the Illustrator

FABRICIO SUAREZ, a recipient of the David Rhodes Scholarship Award for excellence in fine art graduated with a B.F.A in illustration from the School of Visual Arts in New York, New York. In his spare time, he collects artifacts for sculptures. Fabricio lives and works in Jersey City, New Jersey.

"Intelligence plus character is the goal of true education."
Dr. Martin Luther King, Jr.